The World Th
and Other S

An Anthology of work written by
Spark Young Writers
during 2021 - 2022

COPYRIGHT

Spark Young Writers is a Project of
Writing West Midlands

Edited by William Gallagher

With thanks to:
All the Spark Lead and Assistant Writers
The Spark Young Writers
&
The Spark Team at WWM

About Writing West Midlands

Writing West Midlands is the literature development agency for the West Midlands region of the UK. We run events and activities for writers and readers, including our annual Birmingham Literature Festival. We also run Spark Young Writers, which is a major programme of work for young writers aged 8 to 16+ including regular workshops, a summer school and a magazine. Writing West Midlands also works with libraries, publishers and universities to help creative writers develop their skills.

INTRODUCTION

Spark Young Writers is proud to present *The World That I Know*: an Anthology of writing by the young people who make up our Spark Young Writers groups.

At Spark Young Writers we are constantly seeking opportunities for young writers to experience the many aspects of life as a writer. We run an annual conference where we showcase all the varied areas of work connected with writing and respond where we can to the interests of the young writers' we work with by putting on ad-hoc events and signposting other opportunities to our community.

Magazines are often the gateway for emerging writers to find their style and establish themselves as a writer. To give a taste of this, we produce a professionally edited magazine twice a year, where every piece that is submitted receives constructive feedback – even if they have been unsuccessful. Any young writer (aged 8 – 21) living or studying in the West Midlands can submit their work for consideration. See sparkwriters.org/get-involved for more details.

Due to Covid, these groups have largely met online – although we were pleased to end the year running three in person groups. We have big plans for in-person groups in 2022-23.

Our Spark groups are led by professional writers, with the assistance of a volunteer. Each group is run differently and responds to the interests of the participants, but they are invited to try out a wide variety of writing styles that they may not have even thought about before – way beyond poetry and short story writing which they are exposed to at school.

We invited our young writers to submit a piece of writing that they were particularly pleased with which they had begun at one of the sessions they attended during the year. Some of our groups worked on a piece of writing collectively and others are individually written.

We hope you enjoy the range, breadth and scope of the writing included.

Emma Boniwell
Learning & Participation Manager
Writing West Midlands

With thanks to our funders Arts Council England

Spark Young Writers 2021-2022

Each Spark Young Writers group is run by a lead writer with an assistant.

For 2021-2022, the lead writers were:

Junior Birmingham: Helen Calcutt

Junior Walsall: Mandy Ross

Junior South: Emilie Lauren Jones

Junior Online: Sara-Jane Arbury

Teen Burton: Maria Whatton

Teen South West: Ken Preston

Teen South East: Aoife Mannix

Teen Black Country: Emma Purshouse

Teen Online: William Gallagher

Teen Birmingham: Lorna French

The assistant writers were: Katie Hook, Athiya Subani, Fiona Harding, Shani Patel, Laura Whetton, Greg Dimmock, Will Smith, Marlene Anzengruber, Fizra Bibi, Leela Doherty, Maddy Clark, Emily Edge, Charlotte Goodger

COLLECTIVE WRITING

Some of our groups decided to write
pieces together

Who We Are

by the Writing West Midlands Junior Online Spark Group

I am a storm, unpredictable, and always ready to strike.

I am the living room table. I constantly make my brother stub his toe.

I am a white fluffy cloud, accompanying the bright, golden sun, but when I suffer, you will suffer too, for I am also a rain cloud, spreading misery around. Darkening the innocent baby-blue skies.

I am an unidentified bulb, mysterious, hidden. No one pays much attention to me now, but perhaps I will bloom some day.

I am warm, pleasant sunshine on a spring day, beaming my bright, warming light to everyone around me.

I am a clumsy Labrador, waiting for cuddles on my owner's grey couch, and a chance to make someone smile.

I am lightning, striking when I am angry. Sometimes I am loud, sometimes I am quiet.

I am a comfy pair of shoes with polished but battered leather and thick laces.

I am a toucan splashing in the rain, while squawking to other birds.

I am a supersonic falcon, stalking its prey in the dead of night.

Celebrating the Commonwealth Games
Spark South Group Poem by Naveen and Molly

As the ball rips through the air,
bat in hand, hitting through
proving success,
it flies like an elegant bird,
it bounces several times
before rolling to the other side.

As the wooden pieces brush along your fingers, hands
shivering,
    the clock counting but finally you hear its last ticks...
    the taste of pure victory runs down your spine
    you emerge crowned the winner.

The pop of a ball off a racquet,
see people having fun,
smashing the ball at your opponent.
You can almost taste the happiness
pulsing through your blood.
Feel the soft fur of a sphere
just soft and always that way –
this is tennis!

Your blood rushing through your veins like a torrent
as you dive
propelling your way to the finish
rushing to victory.

Spark!

by Esme, Tafara and Zaynab,
Walsall Spark young writers' group

Spark! Like striking a match,
an idea starts small,
a quick spark like a moment's star,
Spark grows, flows, trembles, flickers,
flame dances, touches the candle,
and look! The wick shines hot gold bright light.
Spark! Writing together,
start small, sharing ideas,
exploring, adventuring, imagining, remembering
experience, dreams, places you've been.
Ideas grow, flow, tremble, flicker
minds building, brains set alight.
Spark our minds into realising
we can embrace a new power –
and look! New stories birthed.

POEMS

The World That I Know
by Doroti Polgar, Teen Online Group

There is a world that I know, and it is a world
of love, a world of hate, a world of miracles and pain.
There is a world that I know because of everything I have seen,
and all the people I have known – and I know

a man who shops from the past-sell-by date stall
and leaves a plate of dinner for a stranger to take,
because he knows how hard it can be for a mother
to feed her children from the little she makes in a day.

I know a father who buried his daughter at twenty
because there was a shortage of donors
when there should have been plenty,
if only more people had the courage to speak.

I know a child who is abused by his peers on his way to school,
the names they call and the bruises they force.
They create a war which he can't fight, let alone win,
all because of the colour of his skin.

I know a woman who dreams of getting married
of having children, of starting a family.
But the dream seems so distant that she no longer speaks about
it at all,
    because in her country marrying another woman is against the
law.

I know a nurse who works hours and hours and hours past his
shift

because he watched a child battle biased odds and live.
He gives and cares until the skin peels from his hands
yet we stare and we question because the nurse is a man.

I know a girl who reads books about women's history,
she walks her own hometown streets in fear,
and questions: has society for girls really improved?
Or has the bad been put under cover by a modern
        brand of shoes?

I know a boy who grew up in a broken family,
he finds comfort in a singer's lyrics about absent daddies.
Now, he treats his wife and children with love and respect,
keeping the promise to his younger self to never
        repeat that cycle again.

I know a couple who worked from debt to Disneyland
for their two children.
They gave up their dream to give them a chance;
they put a hold on their plans and pressed pause on the dance.

I know a teacher whose mother left school at fourteen.
Her students don't listen, but she never gives in,
she persists and persists
because her mother has taught her that education is a gift.

I know a man who is a celebrated actor by name
but his heart has never changed from when he
was that little boy, dreaming by night and working by day.
He cares more for the ones he loves than he ever could
        for his fame.

I know a girl who lives her life in silence
not because she was born without the ability to hear
but because the world around her is choosing not to
	learn the language of sign.
They don't realise that the disability lies not in the
	individual but in our society.

And I know a man who took his own life,
who may still be here if people listened to help
more than the funeral eulogy his broken-hearted mother
	had to prepare.
If only people started to care before he was dead.

There is a world that I know, and it is a
world of love, a world of hate, a world of miracles and pain.
There is a world that I know because of everything I've seen,
and all the people I have known.
And I know that there is so much in this world that I am
	yet to know,
so much that we may never know, but
one thing we must know is that we are only ever a kind
	word away from seeing a little more,
and shaping each other's worlds closer to the world we
	all wish we would know.

Why I Write
by Chloe Pick, Teen Online Group

Fly free as a cloud
Never touch the ground
I am untethered
Words flowing out of my fingers
Ink running through my blood
I don't ask why me
I just let the words take control
The truest form of who I am
And what tales I want to tell
Staring back at me

What once was a blank page
Now overrun with monsters and castles
Dragons and fairies
A hope that everything will be better in the future
A hope that a new world is never more than a bookshop away
A world that other people can get lost in
And find sanctuary within the covers of a book
As they laugh, cry, and sit on the edge of their seats
Wondering what will happen next

That is why I write
To show my inner thoughts and feelings
To show how I wish the world could be
To fly free as a cloud
Never touching the ground

Two sides to every story
by Krishan Nayyar, Birmingham Junior Group

Happiness is sometimes sad
Happiness comes in many shapes and sizes .
Happiness can be deep or shallow .
Happiness is a decision we make

Sadness may creep up on you
Sadness can be black and dark
Sadness can be shared or personal
Sadness stains our heart

Neither can be avoided
Neither are what we expected
Neither leave us alone
Neither last forever

Both are part of being human
Both give us reasons to live
Both bookmark our soul
Both shape our lives

A Better Outlook
by Amelie Baker, Teen Online Group

The sea's waves crash,
violent and vicious.

The sky's clouds rumble,
grey and grumpy.

The tree's branches rustle,
clumsy and chaotic.

The storm threatens,
adamant and audacious.

Still,
the Sun shines through,
Hope.

Contentment
by Samuel Parbutt, Junior Online Group

Contentment is a small sparrow splashing around in a puddle
and pecking at the orange blossom blooms.

Contentment is a sunny day with frost on the road –
so fresh it puts a spring in your step.

Contentment is that fern uncoiling in spring
to spread its fronds around the woodland.

Contentment is your favourite pair of fluffy socks
that keep your feet toasty on a winter's day.

Contentment is a lunchtime where everyone gathers around
    the table
for warm soup and a thick slice of bread.

Contentment is home, a place to relax and feel good.

Contentment is orange, the colour of light and relaxation.

Ode To My Glasses
by Feranmi Ogunmiluyi, Junior Online Group

Oh glasses, sweet glasses!
Whatever would I do without you?
You sit perfectly on my face and without you, I am blind!
I would walk into lampposts like a clumsy oaf.
From the moment I walked into Specsavers,
I knew that I needed you.
Without caring for the price,
I discarded the fakes and frauds who tried to replace you.
After TEN WHOLE MINUTES, you were finally mine.
I barely remember my past life before you.
Finally, I am complete. Indestructible.
If a bird plucked you off my face, I would chase it
      back to its nest.

O glasses, I cannot live without you.
When your loving help is not with me, I am blind.
With you, we are unstoppable.

You cannot be replaced; your love is too kind to be substituted.

I wake up in the morning vacant.
Then I see you, and my heart fills with joy.

Ode To Pizza
by Abigail Higgott, Junior Online Group

O my dear, beloved pizza,
how I simply ADORE you.
You are the one thing that demolishes my hunger,
the one thing that gives me something to eat
when I'm watching horror films.
When I become scared at the movie,
you make me feel joyous once more, like a power.
I would be in the depths of deepest despair without you.
You are only one amazing click away,
and when you arrive at my door, it melts my heart
like the oozing, succulent cheese that drips off your edges.
That first bite makes all my worry and sadness burn away
like the oven you sleep in, and that's why I treasure you.
O, what would I do without you pizza?
I would be in the deepest, darkest depths of despair,
dark like the colour of your crust when you burn.
The exquisite taste you have, takes nothing to learn.

Loneliness
by Feranmi Ogunmiluyi, Junior Online Group

Loneliness is a leaf, snatched away from the
comfort of the tree,
trampled on by giants who pass.

Loneliness is a chair, enslaved to carry the
burdens of others and itself.

Loneliness is a fish in the sea, separated from
its brothers and sisters by a net,
and slowly being dragged towards the surface.

Loneliness is a run-down warehouse, smashed windows,
never to be used again.

Loneliness is an unbreakable bubble of despair around you,
keeping you from your friends and family.

Loneliness is a realm of shadows, fear and darkness,
sending you spiralling through hate and swallowing you whole.

Loneliness wants to be love, but alas, cannot grasp it
as it trickles through its fingers like sand.

The Prison Cell
by Liang Zi Zhao, Junior Online Group

I stand there in utter misery,
Every day, criminals come but don't go
They are locked behind my dirty, decaying walls,
Why was I chosen to be this?

They bang and scratch tallies into my walls,
Not knowing that I'm wincing in pain,
I plead and plead for them to stop,
But those heartless creatures take no notice.

Why wasn't I born a palace like my friend Buckingham?
Why couldn't I be cared for and polished like good old Eiffel?
Why couldn't I be an antique like Colosseum?
WHY WAS I THIS STUPID PRISON?

Another day of pure agony,
More officers come with offenders.
I thought, Of course
Surely the officers would listen.

They didn't pay any attention,
Why was everyone in this world so rude?
Humans, such ignorant creatures.
At least, I wasn't one of them.

Suddenly, officers flood in,
Freeing and grabbing the lawbreakers.
I see from my eyes outside, another building

That looks just like me.

Hooray, I yell in happiness,
I finally have some peace,
I stand here lonely but content,
I no longer suffer like before.
I'm no longer a shelter for breakers of the law.

Reminiscence of an Aged Castle

by William Tingley, Junior Online Group

I stand in shame, embarrassment and disgrace
as strangers infiltrate my once strong walls,
now tattered shards.

Alas, it seems my days are done.
My folk, my people lost,
just memories of old.

Who am I to blame now, for disrespect and death?
Those who uttered words of woe are rolling in the grave.

But now look at me, plagued by petty fools.
These "tourists" who haunt me come forth
    with looks of pleasure,
cursing me with this "re-establishment."

I stand alone, bitter for my loss.
It dawns upon me that when my time comes,
I, and my folk of old, will all be reduced to legend.

My Brother And Me
by Uthaymin Ahmed, Junior Online Group

I am a seagull squawking at the window
when my brother tries to sleep.

I am the living room table,
constantly making my brother stub his toe.

I am a thorn on a rose,
making my brother prick himself.

I am a belt,
I always hide when my brother needs me.

I am a very nice Porsche,
but when my brother saves up to buy me the price goes up
      so he can't afford me.

Our Globe
by Samuel Parbutt, Junior Online Group

Ominous as it seems
Under Earth's sphere of gas
Roots are set, no matter how many trees we slice down.

Grow, nature will grow back.
Listen to the Earth.
Or if our situation gets worse, we will all go down.
But if we do clean up our Earth,
Everyone will be happy.

Shame
by William Tingley, Junior Online Group

Shame is a humble flower,
decisions, places, events, may cause it to wilt.

Shame is a bird of prey, choosing to fly alone,
lessening its burden.

Shame is a violent storm, sweeping through walls and roofs,
whittling them down to bricks and mortar.

Shame is a childhood book, tucked in the corner of a shelf,
reflecting upon its moment of glory.

Shame is a great cliff, looming over you,
a barrier you must overcome.

Revenge
by Uthaymin Ahmed, Junior Online Group

Revenge is war, getting shot by your opponent and waiting to
strike back.

Revenge is a tiger tumbling through the woods after prey.

Revenge is a seagull stealing chips from someone because that
someone shooed
    the seagull off their lawn and the seagull has a good memory
    so it knows whose chips are gonna get stolen.

Revenge is a lightning storm, blocking the sun to ruin
everyone's day.

Loneliness
by Abigail Higgott, Junior Online Group

Loneliness is a beaten, battered teddy bear stuck in a cold, grubby charity shop, his only companion the bright, silver moon blazing through the greasy, smeared window.

Loneliness is a small, whimpering panda cub in a smoky, dirty landfill,
    which once used to be his home.

Loneliness is a dusty, untouched piano in the corner of a large, grand living room,
    its keys buckled and broken.

Loneliness is a tall, foggy hill, looming above a lively, bustling town,
    with nothing but a dead oak tree on its surface.

Loneliness is a pair of worn, scruffy shoes in the darkness of the wardrobe,
    too small for their owner, unpolished, no care like they used to have.

Trees

by Temilolaoluwa Olaiya, Black Country Teen Online

We all need trees to grow, for the young and the old.
One of my many desires is to see the trees grow higher.
Grab a small tiny seed, these are all the things we need:
Dig a hole with a pup, add a seed and watch it shoot up high.
We all need trees to grow, for the young and the old.

Joy
by Ealingee Rajeevan, Junior Online Group

Joy is a dog barking happily at its owner coming home from work.

Joy is the glorious sun shining down over everyone,
watching people from around the world smiling and jumping.

Joy is the afternoon, when pupils come home from school and play with their friends.

Joy is the park, where children swing, slide and smile.

Joy is yellow, the colour of happiness and the sun.

Guilt

by Liang Zi Zhao, Junior Online Group

Guilt is a bright spotlight following you everywhere.
Guilt is a painful thorn that clings on to you.
It is an inescapable, uncomfortable containment,
Or a hauntingly familiar pigeon that pecks you,
When you've only just reached contentment.

You try as hard as you can to escape,
But guilt is like your looming shadow.
You always try and try to pull free,
But it's glued to your foot and you know.
It's an invisible thing that you can't see.

It squashes its way into your house,
And in your brain, it starts to mess about.
It's hard to focus with it in your head,
And all you want to do is stay in bed.
You feel hopeless for you alone can't fight it.

You feel so sad to the core,
But don't worry, forgiveness is the cure.

Freedoms
by Uma Ahluwalia, Teen Online Group

Imagine having all of your freedoms taken away,
Trapped in a basement in Mariupol,
Untouched by the light of day,
Can't leave your home, can't wash,
Afraid to express your opinion.
Imagine forgetting the way to your school,
Which you once travelled every single day,
And what of your future?
Imagine your daily routine is wake up, wait, sleep,
You only have one toy to hug at night,
But it will never replace a hug from your father.

The Bewitched Witch
by Zaynab Baksh, Walsall Junior Group

There once was a
boy,
His name was
Roy,
He was rich,
And he lived with a witch,
Who had a black cat,
Who always wanted a pat,

Roy's father was so weak,
He couldn't even speak,
The witch said she could cure him,
But all she had done was make him grim,
Roy didn't like the witch,
She was creepy and bewitched,
One day she just left,
And Roy was in his best

The Monopoly Run
by Zaynab Baksh, Walsall Junior Group

One day we went on a run,
A monopoly run,

We went with scouts,
And we took loads of routes,
The run was in London,
We had a lot of fun,
While we raced around,

We took a Tube,
and a couple of buses,

By the end of the run,
We were drained,
While we were on the coach,
We found out,
That we had won,
Hooray!

Share
by Temilolaoluwa Olaiya, Black Country Teen Online

Make sure you always share
At home and everywhere
Share a toy, share a friend so your fun never ends
Share a smile, share a wish, so your friendship is never
squished.
Share s hug, share a kiss so you will find lots of bliss
Make sure you always share
At home and everywhere

PROSE

The Shot
by Chloe Pick, Teen Online Group

It was all over the news. The whole town knew what had
happened. No one knew how it had happened, but it had
happened so everyone had to live with it now. Everyone knew
what had happened when the shot was fired and the police
inspector fell. Everyone seemed to know how long it had taken for
the man to stop breathing but no one knew how long it took for
the murderer to flee. No one had stopped to look when a man ran
through the town, covered in blood. And no one had cared when
an anonymous fund for the family was set up, when an
anonymous body was buried, the gravestone simply quoting 'Love
is blind; friendship closes its eyes.'.

No one batted an eye 12 years later when the gravestone was
removed, the body dug up. But Nathan Brown noticed. He had
grown up being told that true friends would stab you in the front,
as only they would be that honest. He was 5 and had always been
told that you should never help anyone, lest they want to repay
you in some way. You had to only look out for yourself and no
one else. Otherwise you would become an anonymous grave in a
small village, your grave dug up. Leave debts behind you, they
would soon come back to you. Nathan never questioned this. Why
would he? His father was a police inspector and never lied.
Therefore whatever Nathan was told must be true.

He was only 10 when he saw his world for what it was. He was
stuck in a glass cage. He could see out enough that he thought he
was free but he was at the mercy of all those who watched him.
He began to observe the other children in his town. They all still
believed what they were told. If someone fell over in the
playground, that was their problem. If the police searched your
home, then you just had to deal with it. You couldn't ever stand

up for yourself. Everything they said was true. Everything was safe in their town because of them. No one had questioned when the police had seized control of the village 18 years ago, when the police inspector had fell.

The old police inspector had served well but it was time for change. That was when Nathan's father had taken over. He still lived in the town and regularly spoke in the local school. He never answered any questions though. He knew the children had been told about how to never leave debts behind them. he knew the best out of them all. He had shot someone once. It was an action that could never be repaid. The victim lay below an anonymous grave. His police badge still shone under the ground.

Everyone knew what had happened the day the old police inspector stood down. No one ever questioned why the shot was fired.

Dearest Thaiyaji
by Krishan Nayyar, Birmingham Junior Group

I'm not sure what to say but I need to let you know that I miss you. I know we didn't spend lots of time together and I was always more interested in playing with Ekisha, but that's because I expected you to always be there. I didn't think I had to pay attention each time I saw you as we had so many times to talk in the future. I'm sorry that I didn't relish each minute.

There are memories of us together I'll hold dear forever, like the kebab conversations and the little pair of shoes you went yourself to buy for me that are in my room. You were an amazing big brother to my daddy and I promise to try to be the same to Ekisha.

I didn't really understand why I was so sad at first. There's not lots and lots of memories for me to talk about like Jovan does, we didn't see each other every day like you and Daddy. Im my life there's nothing really that's changed each day since you passed, so why do I feel so sad?

Mummy and I talked and I realised what it is. I'm missing the future that should have been ours. My sadness is for when I want to ask you for advice about relationships. You sneaking me a drink without mummy knowing. You asking me to keep an eye on Ekisha on a night out. Showing you my first car. Joking about how you're becoming an old man. Treating you to a meal with my first pay check. The stag do you would've organised for me. Showing you round my first house. You holding my children as the funnest Baba in the world (Daddy will be great but you've always been the funnier one). I'm sorry that each of these things we won't have together and so many other things, and that's why I feel so sad. I also know my Daddy will miss you lots and I worry about him.

I promise that I'll hold you in my heart and remember you. I'll try to be supportive for Daddy and I'll always be there if Ekisha needs me.

Rest in peace

Room In New York
by Evie Hodgetts, South West Teen Online Group

Rustling his newspapers, he focused on the tiny print on the page, trying not to let the ink dye his sweaty fingertips. She wiped dust off the piano keys with her slender fingers, swallowing the urge to sneeze. She began to methodically hit the keys with one finger, going up and down in a simple, slow, choppy scale: C, D, E, F, G, A, B.

It made a dull, flat sound, filling the stuffy, silent room with noise. She swivelled around so she was sat at the piano properly. Her right arm was stiff - it had been leaning against the polished coffee table in an awkward position.

There was an indent in her skin and a patch of redness from where the circular edge had dug into her soft, pale skin. Pushing one of the pedals down, she hit the keys with more aggression than she had before, the sound becoming even uglier. She sighed, turning back around.

"What would you like for dinner, Harry?" she asked.

"Yes, dear," he replied, not looking up.

She paused.

"It wasn't a yes or no question."

Up, Up North
by Bridey Bingley, South East Teen Online Group

I'm going to pack my bags and go up North. Of course I won't really, but they'll all think I had. I might as well have.

And then my husband will die.

I'll be up, up North though. The police will call me. And what a tragedy that my husband was murdered in his sleep, shot in the head, blood staining the white, crisp sheets in sticky pools. All while I was up, up North.

And whilst I won't be there I can picture it perfectly. I can picture exactly how the murderer would do it. My husband would be sleeping. It's easier to kill people when they're sleeping. Not that I have experience, of course. It's just common sense.

My husband never sleeps better than when he's drunk on wine. So the murderer will make him dinner and pour them both a glass of wine. And the murderer will put the bottle on the table. The meal will be suffocating for the murderer, as every meal is. My husband is always so stifling. The affair with the murderer's sister will sit heavily between them. My husband will have another glass to ease his nerves. And another. By the time he makes it up to bed he will be fast asleep. The murderer will be waiting in their room, waiting for the soft sound of snores. The murderer will reach under their pillow for the cold, hard metal of the gun and their feet will pad on the carpeted hallway and my husband's door will creak open and the murderer will creep inside. The gun will be a heavy weight in their hand as they watch my husband sleeping. They'll place a gloved finger on the trigger and then -

Well, I'll be up, up North and the police will call.

Though I won't be there, I know the murderer will cover up the crime too. It will be bin day early the next morning. And so the gun will be shoved in a Tesco carrier bag with the rest of the rubbish and the disposable gloves. It will be far away by the time the police arrive. It will be my husband's day off, after all. No one will notice he's gone until the evening. The murderer will climb up the trellis, added two months prior, and so conveniently placed. It will be all too easy for them to smash the window inwards.

So the police will call and I'll be up, up North and they can't find the gun and my husband's bedroom was broken into – that pesky trellis – and no, I can't think of anyone who wanted my husband dead.

Except me, of course.

But I won't say that. It's not relevant to the investigation. After all, I was up, up North.

Mercurial
by Charlotte Wain, Burton Teen Group

If we were to dispose the world of monsters, few would be left. The saints are innocent… you'd think so, wouldn't you?

You see, monsters are inside every living being. Only some can overcome their demons, while others are enveloped in greed, devious, malicious behaviour. It's a shame, really, that you cannot see into souls, observe their every thought, every action made. Then you would have factions of who and who wasn't worthy of purity.

Perhaps then you would realise that not all heroes are saviours and that the villainous are not always portrayed in the way they should be.

That is just how life evolves.

Everything passes, nothing is forever, revelation comes just at the finale.

Crows circle over a large, ancient, rustic construction. Cracked roof tiles, a large triangular point above the entrance. The structure was stained in variations from white to orange. Dead grass and a spindly singular tree guarded it. Moss and corpses of nature entwined within. A tall woman with her hair strained back in a sleek ponytail. Her face was geometric, sharp and strict. She held a jet black notebook, the shade identical to her hair and clothing. Her figure was anonymous. Her clothing masked it. Despite this her features were distinguished and ornate. Her facial features were furthermore masked in a similar way. A black mask and deep break rectangular sunglasses.

The anonymous woman looked back to the construction that she had previously vacated. The hundreds of crows had disappeared, few were seen hastily flying into the horizon.

The woman's heart swelled, demonstrated by her slight lift of facial structure; mainly in her cheeks, the small yet noticeable wrinkles sparkling near her eyes.

The crescent moon had just about reached its dominant point in the blue shades of void and mystery. It erupted gradually into a paint brush, smothering the skies with harmonious shades.

The woman took a step through a small, sparkling puddle, enveloped ripples and several, various multiple specks of dust and dirt. Her legs navigated her through a deserted, baron pathway towards apologies, away from the ancient construction of rubble and bricks, away from the crumbling structure.

The woman striding away to discover a new life for herself. To explore the possibilities the earth had to offer. Snatching her past and vigorously throwing it behind her, where all bad things belong. She had finally escaped a life of being an ambushed, captured attendant – no longer a toy to be thrown around and used as a villain's puppet.

The Reindeer Rock
by Ealingee Rajeevan, Junior Online Group

Max, a black Labrador, had his once-a-month leave for a whole day. It was nice and sunny, so he decided to sunbathe for a bit. Meanwhile, the weather became more intense. The clouds turned grey and fog started to shroud the air. When Max woke up, it was raining cats and dogs.

Frantically, Max ran to Reindeer Rock to check that he was okay. Reindeer Rock was a large stone born from a volcano. It looked like a reindeer but could walk and talk. But when Max got there, Dr Lotsishots, an evil villain, was deviously grabbing the baby Reindeer Rock egg!

The Doctor said, "Hmmm... this looks like a good specimen for crossbreeding, red thorns and a green, fuzzy outer layer. I've never saw anything like this before."

Accidentally, Dr Lotsishots dropped a clue and ran back to his lab without looking back. He placed the egg with his jars of crossbreeding materials and went to bed.

Max thought he would never see Reindeer Rock, his BFF, ever again. Then, he heard a voice. He exclaimed, "Oh dear Reindeer, you're back!"

"Hi Max, I'm glad to see you, but where's my egg?" said Reindeer.

"It's where you left it, Reindeer," replied Max.

They went to check, but there was no trace of the egg to be seen. As they climbed down a tree, they suddenly saw a playing card on the ground. It had a syringe on it and the letters "stohsistoL rD". They had no idea what it meant, so they decided to go to the Puzzle Lord.

First, Max and Reindeer had a slumber. Then they travelled to Tiles Master forest. When they approached the Puzzle Cave, a voice said "Who goes there?"

"Reindeer Rock and Max," they replied.

As they entered the facility, they saw a nest and gently tapped the shoulder of the Puzzle Lord, who was a small, very smart, hedgehog. They interrogated him.

"Who sent this card?"

The Puzzle Lord replied, "It was Dr Lotsishots."

"Ugh, not him again!" said Max and Reindeer in unison. They had encountered the Doctor before, when he had tried to steal a precious meteor from space.

They said thanks to the Puzzle Master, and went to find the Doctor's Laboratory. When they got there, it was only 5am, and everyone was in a deep sleep. Dr Lotsishots had left the front door ajar, so they tiptoed in, unnoticed.

On his desk, was the egg! They just had to nab it and make a run for it. But then, the laser system activated. They could be disintegrated! They managed to avoid all the dangerous lasers until...

The Adventure of the Magical Dressing Gown
By Ari Virk Nicholl, Birmingham Junior Group

One frosty, freezing day in a small house Jake, a bored boy with a wild imagination in isolation, sat in bed looking at his Beatles' Yellow Submarine dressing gown, then suddenly a florescent gold and yellow shiny light shone out - he Jumped out of bed and into his blue dressing gown that has the yellow submarine embroidered on it. Suddenly he was sat down inside a Yellow Submarine Time Machine travelling through time to the 1970s. As he flew he also saw some other yellow submarines with people inside them waving at him. He saw flying past him some colourful fish as well.

Jake was feeling really pleased with his adventure so far. Then he had a rough, bumpy landing on the grass of... Pepper Land where he met his favourite group, The Beatles doing a concert in Pepper Land playing a variety of brass instruments. A crazy colourful land of flying fish and peppers that look like crocodiles and the four faces of The Beatles are carved into the huge mountains of Pepper Land.

A cruel Blue Meanie giant stomped over and watched whilst The Beatles sang "Hello Goodbye", Jake's favourite song. The Blue Meanie felt fiercely annoyed and jealous of everyone having fun whilst he was having none! Out of nowhere the Blue Meanie attacked everyone with his giant foot and his humongous arms. The Beatles and Jake ran scared and hid behind the huge colourful mountains.

The blue meanie giant found them and picked them up, but The Beatles cleverly balanced on the Blue Meanies nose with scared Jake with them. They jumped up and down on the flying fish to escape. Luckily, they jumped so high off the flying fish that The Beatles and Jake managed to climb into the yellow submarine and there they happily sang "All you need is love" all the way back to Jake's house. Jake was sad to see them leave but said thank you for the magical adventure.

Then the Beatles flew off in the yellow submarine singing "We all live in a Yellow Submarine" all the way back to Pepper Land.

Jake never felt bored again and he even asked his mum to buy different dressing gowns for his birthday, to see what other lands are in them!

The Inheritance
By Ari Virk Nicholl, Birmingham Junior Group

I walked down the stairs to the shivering sand of Dundoirp's coastal shoreline, known for the most threatening climate in the Netherlands, Europe and even the world. As I trudged defiantly down the coastal bay, I saw black speckles in the distant horizon. I walked and walked until I found the black speckle was a mysterious cave in the sea, with a passageway leading into darkness, I looked around and thought to myself should I go in there?

In a split second, I thought I should enter, as there must be treasure and gold there because in my beloved middle-aged mansion down in the bunker hangs a picture of my great, great, great, great, great grandfather William the Great, that shows him stood outside this very cave, holding emeralds, rubies and more, that have never been inherited by me. So I'm taking it all! Or I could just be mistaken, and it could be just a damp, dewy middle-aged coal passage. I poked my head though but there was nothing. Panicking. I walked along that same passageway. I saw glitter. I ran down as that sparkle looked bigger and brighter than before. Several steps later, I came across a winding, slippery trail. I stepped on it, suddenly, it lit up, it was bright gold, I was off slipping down this flawless, golden trail.

There it was! A field of gold, red, green, and blue precious stones. I sprang on to the rubies first and plunged them into my pockets, I grabbed the gold and gathered it under my vest, scooped my hat along the sapphires and gathered the emeralds in my empty shoes. I was filled with delight. I felt I got what I deserved.

The only question now was, how to get out?

It looked like I was at the bottom of a chasm, if there was an end to it. I'd forgot my glue gun, but I could melt bronze to form a ladder, or could I use the gritty sharp bronze to make a firm passageway. I decided to make the firm passage as I didn't know where the ladder would lead to. It took me several hours, but when I looked to the finished passageway it had vanished into hard iron like granite rock. I felt furious at myself, but then I thought, am I trapped? The only way out now was making the bronze ladder and I wasn't sure if I should climb up the ladder or if I should just sleep here for the night. In the end I decided I must climb it and take my treasure with me.

I was so close to the entrance of the light, but when I climbed the very last step the ladder melted and crumbled down and at that moment all my valuable stones suddenly exploded, and I came crashing back down to the surface and into the water.

I knew I would never get out ever again, then I slept into nothingness.

A Diary For My Cousin So She Knows
What She Has Missed
by Maariyah Baksh, Teen Online Group

Dear Cousin,

As you can see my hand writing is quite wobbly, that is because
YOU HAVE JUST BEEN BORN! We haven't got a picture of
you yet because you have been taken to be bathed and everything
has happened rather quickly. Nana (our grandfather) was crying
hysterically because I quote, "I'm emotional because my bheti
(daughter) has been through a lot of pain."

Nani (grandmother) is also crying. Right now Nana has that
typical look on his face that he gets when he is on WhatsApp as he
is texting relatives about your birth. As you can see this is the
beginning of me changing your nappies as your mum and my
mum say that I HAVE to do it. My mum was crying too it was
like a crying party although it should have been a happy one.
Adults! (Sigh). My hand is starting to hurt, so I'll say bye now.

From Maariyah, the eldest one.

Scream Like No-One's Listening
by Sophie Nock, Teen Online Group

A scream echoes through mildewed corridors. A person's in trouble, you might be thinking. Somebody help them! But no-one comes. No-one cares. No-one ever has, and no-one ever will.

The doors in this place are off their hinges; leaning against the wall; propped up in doorframes; lying side by side in a long-forgotten attic. The floor wears moss like carpet. Damp patches and peeling paper are coats for the tired walls, jealously guarding them against the winter wind.

The scream comes again. The very same scream.

But someone must care? you're surely thinking. There must be someone?

You're wrong. The scream echoes again, over and over – the very same scream each time, same timbre, same volume, wherever the listener is in the rabbit-warren building. Somehow, it is identical.

Every. Single. Time.

The corridors twist and turn, and the listener who treads the darkened halls full of empty doorways and small, cracked windows with bars in their frames finds themselves back where they were before, again and again.

This time the scream is different. It is the listener, lost and wandering among the empty halls that echo with old, weary cries. Someone help them! I can feel you thinking now. Somebody must be there; they have to get them out. No-one cared about the last scream; why should anyone care about this one? There's no-one there anyway, no-one but the listener; shrieking as the sky darkens outside. The listener, nameless, faceless, does not think they can survive a night in here. Many have thought so.

You see, this was once an asylum. A place that drowned in anguish, night and day; where sleep was an impossibility in the face of looming nightmares and dark corners where clawed monsters waited; cruel men who called themselves doctors, stalking forward, syringes in hands.

Not one inmate here believed they would survive the night.

Even back then, their howls were ignored. The rotted wooden trays and rusty buckets are the only sign now that these people once had gaolers; people who might have listened, could have cared... but didn't. The listener cannot bear the sight of those buckets, rimmed in blood-red rust. There are no blankets here, the iron frames of the beds cold and hard, no mattresses in sight.

The corridors are endless, looping. They go on forever, round and round, never to be escaped. The listener is lost, still listening to that long-ago plea that echoes through time, caught in the ancient walls and blocked-up chimneys, the final scream of the final inmate before the final doctor wheeled that final body away.

Echoing again

  and again

    and again.

The listener screams one last time, a scared and sad reply to the mournful cry of a woman long lost.

All that echoes now is silence.

The listener sits, back pressed to the tired wall, staring up through the bars of the tiny window in the cell they have chosen. Nameless, faceless. Voiceless.

No-one is coming, they realise now.

No-one cares. No-one ever has.

Not me, and not you. Not really.

No-one comes, because this is an asylum: your screams mean nothing.

Darkhouse
by Sophie Nock, Teen Online Group

It is dark outside. The wind is screaming through the broken shutters and forcing them together, then apart, together, apart – a chaotic couple, half alive, part joyous and all insane. On the other side of the window, the salt spray spots them dark, until the spots are too close and too thick for the worn blue paint and old yellow flower patterns beneath to be seen. The hinges look like they can't hold on much longer.

Across the cliffs, the lighthouse is dark; the lantern in the high, glass-walled room should be lit by now. People out on the water need its light. My mind is caught by the image of a rusted skeleton ship, crewed by phantom mariners and water-sprites of broken glass and bubbles, deep beneath the sea. Unseen, and angry. Angry at the old lighthouse keeper who has forgotten to light the lantern.

Of course, he'll be long dead by then; instead, I'll be the only one left for the returned ghosts to blame. But, no-one cares about my well-being, do they? The wind rushes in through the gap under the door and extinguishes one of my candles. The electricity is out and they're my only light.

I'm terrified now. I'm not having barnacled skeletons coming after me in fifty years' time to get revenge about this night when I'm the only one left who was around when it happened, by then dementia-ridden and sightless. I'll have to go to the lighthouse, find out what he's doing.

On the waves, the storm will be far worse than it is here. I can see small flashes of lightning like scars at the edge of the dark sky, but out there it will be enormous, stabbing down at sailors like the fork of a vengeful god before he lifts them, caught and perfectly fried, to his grey cloud-lips. An unpleasant thought indeed. To look on the bright side (not that anything is bright tonight), I suppose it does make me glad that I'm not out there, caught in the sudden squall.

For the people who are, though… even if I reach the lighthouse, will they make it?

The moment the door is unlocked, it blows against me, knocking me backwards. My torch flickers, disturbed by the electrical charge in the air. Tell me about it, torch. I think my hair is sticking to the ceiling with the static of it all.

There's not been a storm like this since my grandparents' time.

The rocks are slippery, my feet treacherously unsteady, but if I go up to the road then I'll be too slow. If there are any sailors out there, then if they aren't dead by now they will be soon. The rocks are the quickest way. Sea spray batters my cheeks with the wind. I can hear whispers in the fall of it onto the rocks, in the rush of the waves beneath my feet. Come here, they say, it isn't cold here. You will be warm. The lighthouse is dark; I'm not sure the Keeper's even there. Oh, well. I know ways in. If need be, I will light it myself, though I don't know how.

My torch flickers again, haphazard beams stretching out from my shaking grip. The writhing surface reflects it – here, there, elsewhere – until it goes out, overwhelmed by salt and sea. Useless American piece of kit.

Darkness.

A little light comes from further out to sea, the lightning over the ocean. By its intermittent crashes, I reach the shed where our land borders that of the lighthouse. There is an emergency torch stashed behind a loose brick just next to the door. This one is steady, and brighter than the first. I drop the other, relieved, and move on, pointing the torch at the sodden rocks. When I slip and catch myself, the torch falls from my hands and lands among the jagged pinnacles of rock below. It stares, an all-seeing eye, at the sea. I stare too, but I see nothing.

It is a black mass, uncaring, thrashing against the bounds of gravity. It sucks everything there is far beneath, where water-sprites of broken glass and bubbles, with hair of blood, play. Its song is that of a siren – sweet, on occasion, haunting and beautiful. Now, though, she screams. She cries out in pain and anger, lashing back against the lightning strikes and grasping people instead, wrecking boats, ripping sails.

When I move to pick up my fallen angel of a torch, she grasps me too. Her tortured moan rings in my ears as I turn mid-fall and see the lighthouse: dark, abandoned.

Helpless.

Just like me.

The Haunted Home
by Jennifer-Rose Newey, Birmingham Junior Group

Have you ever been haunted? It's a simple question. You have or you haven't. Well, I certainly know someone who has. Someone you wouldn't expect.

It's mid-morning, Marie and Len Hall have just arrived at 24 Ashfield Crescent (their new home.) Before the move, many people said that they shouldn't have chosen this one particular house, but with them being Halls, they decided to anyway. Once inside, Marie suddenly felt the urge to unpack; whereas Len wanted to get used to the place. So she went upstairs, got her bags and began to unpack. But in a split second, she saw something odd.

Two weeks later, there was a knock at the door. Marie went to answer it. At the door, a man stood there. "Er… hello there. Do you live here?" Marie hesitated a little because she thought that the neighbours would've got a message about new neighbours. "Hey who's there hun?" Len asked. After a sharp look at the man, Len made eye contact with him. "And you are…?" "Thomas. Thomas Willcox. I'm your new neighbour. Well… not for long." Marie and Len both looked at each other confused.

"What do you mean it won't last long?" Marie enquired. But instead of answers, Thomas' rambling just caused more confusion. "Well, for several years now many people have rushed out of the house without looking back. There have been many tails and myths that this home is haunted."

As soon as Thomas said that, Len slammed the door. "He's probably just trying to make us move out of the neighbourhood cause he doesn't like us very much." said Len, but Marie knew something wasn't right.

After this encounter, more odd things began to happen to Marie. At night, she felt like someone was pushing down on the bed when no-one was there. If she put the toilet seat down, it would soon be up again. But worst of all, Len never noticed these things. Whenever she tried to tell Len, he would just say to Marie that it was her mind playing tricks on her. However, Marie knew that something just wasn't right. That's when things got serious.

A few days later, Len went to work and Marie got her laptop ready for the day. As time passed, she was listening to one of her colleagues about taxes and generally boring things. When Marie began to talk, her colleague noticed something in the hallway. "Oh, is that Len by the bathroom?" she questioned. "Erm… no. He is at the hospital and I'm on my own." Marie answered. It was at that moment, she turned around.

I'm Trying Regardless
by Sadeen Ahmad, Teen Online Group

"Someone must've messed the notice board up. Someone must've scribbled my name in jealousy. I don't understand. I can't have not made it. The role was mine. The role was…" Iris's voice broke off as tears fell down her cheek. I watched as she stood on the stage, her throat emitting choking sounds. Her eyes shedding tears. I stood at the corner of the room, daring not to breathe as the echoes of her cries filled the walls. I knew how much Iris wanted the main role. Her whole life depended on it. Her father's not going to let her go without breaking her bones today.

My heart sank as I realised the reality of Iris's living. Having an abusive, drunk father with a hopeless, scared mother. The main lead for Iris was everything. Watching the play today is going to kill her. Her dad even texted her "good luck" but he doesn't know what luck got her. I tugged at my perfectly, seamless dress meant for the main lead in the play, wishing she got it instead and stared at the rags that Iris wore for one of the extras in the play. The man who kills the main lead in an unexpected plot twist of jealousy. Iris will have to fake murder me like we practised countless times with the prop knife.

But then, the crying stopped. Iris wiped her tears and smiled. Then, she started laughing. Laughing hysterically like the funniest joke took place. She started walking closer to the notice board, continuing to laugh maniacally. Laughing like a ring tone that would never end. My body stiffened as I heard her every pitch of her laugh going higher and higher. The poor girl must've gone crazy. Yet my hands gripped together fiercer and I held my breath tighter with every laugh. And deep down behind my broken heart, and fiercely loving soul, was a voice screaming for me to get out of there. A voice screaming to me to run for my life. Yet, I stayed there, my body continuing to curl up in despair.

I watched Iris's reflection from the window. Watched as she pulled out of a knife with residues of blood on it. I held my breath again. What is she doing? That fake knife should be kept away. And there shouldn't be blood on it. No blood on it at all. I then watched as she traced my name next to the word's 'main leader' with the knife. And that was the minute I knew the knife wasn't fake. I heard the movement of the knife screech into the cork board with the blood residue flicking everywhere.

My body lost control and spiralled. I rolled into the drama room hugging my knees. Curled up in denial and horror.

Iris sped round to look at me. Her eyes burning holes into my skin. Her mouth curling at the edges into a smirk. And that was the moment I launched myself up from the floor and ran.

Ran. Ran. Ran. Till I couldn't breathe.

Ran. Ran. Ran. Until I ended up on the floor of the gym stage where everyone was waiting for my arrival. Where everyone was waiting for the moment. The final moment of the play where the jealous boy kills the unwary girl.

The part where Iris kills me. But not like play-pretend.

I try to scuffle backwards, but my feet get trapped in my dress, tangling around and tripping. I look up to see Iris looming above me. Her smirk still not wiped off her face and the knife in her hand. The real knife. The real knife with what she's going to kill me with.

Time stops and my body goes numb. The beating of pounding heart thrusts harder and harder. I scream hysterically and scuffle backwards furiously.

But everyone thinks it's part of the act. Everybody thinks it's my stunning acting that's part of the whole performance. My body goes numb and I feel the cold blade scratching my bare skin.

78

But then, Iris stops. And we both turn to look at the mirror opposite us. Only for us to see one girl staring back.

Iris.

Now the knife is in my hand by my neck and I'm standing up. It was me. There was no other girl. It was just me fighting my screaming mind. It was just me and my mind playing tricks on me. My mind convincing me I could blame and kill someone for not getting the main lead and provoking my father. I drop the knife on the gym stage, the crowd staring back at me, fear glazing over all their faces. I drop down on my knees in realisation of what I almost could've done.

The Rainforest Girl

by Zoë Chapman, Birmingham Junior Group

In the beginning...

There was once a little girl. She was four years old and had grown up in the rainforest. She never know how she had come to live there, but she did know that this was the only place that she would be able to survive.

Though she wasn't very troubled by them, her mind was always full of questions. Questions like: "Why am I here? Who is my mother? How am I expected to live?"

Over time, she began to learn how to live out in the wild, and how to cope.

She made friends with the gorillas, and they made friends with her. And soon enough, they became her family. She grew to be like them: fierce, brave and LOUD.

Once, she found a little gorilla out alone and scared. That is where our story begins.

Jump

She found the baby gorilla and (not having a great imagination) named him Jump. Then, she took him back to the gorilla troop.

"Hmm," said the Chief. "We need to fatten him up, make him stronger. I need a volunteer!"

Only the little girl put her hand up.

[You may be wondering why I keep calling her "the girl". It is because she didn't really have a name. She called herself "Om".]

"Oh, alright then," said the Chief. "If you promise that in all your spare time you will train him and make him strong, then he can live with you."

"I promise!" said Om, eagerly.

"Then he is, from this moment, your gorilla."

Training Jump

Om started training at once. It wasn't as easy as it seemed. The little gorilla would mess about and jump around and not listen. But, on the whole, it wasn't that bad. After a little while, it started to be fun!

Om made sure that every evening, Jump would go to bed with some new knowledge. It seemed to work because they started to have kick-boxing lessons and Jump would always win against Om.

After six months of training, Om presented Jump to the Chief of Gorillas.

"He is strong," said the Chief. "Well done. He is one of us now. Can he fight well?"

"Oh yes!" said Om. She was excited now. She had a little friend, Jump. Jump was excited too: he was finally a big gorilla! He was now part of the big family.

He was free!

SPARK TEEN WRITERS

AGED 12-17?

Join our fun, inspiring sessions for young people who love writing. All sessions are run by professional writers.

Poetry
Playwriting
Fiction
Wordplay

Online and in-person

Saturdays
Monthly from September
2022 – July 2023,
Across the West Midlands
£9 per session

The Exchange,
Centenary Square,
Birmingham
Burton-on-Trent Library
KidderminsterLibrary
Nuneaton Library
Redditch Library
Central Library,
Stoke-on-Trent
Wolverhampton
Art Gallery

Also for younger writers...
Library of Birmingham
The Core, Solihull
New Art Gallery, Walsall
Shrewsbury Art Gallery
and Museum
Belgrade Theatre, Coventry
Hereford Library
The Hive, Worcester

Free places available

for students who receive
Free School Meals
or Pupil Premium.

Booking is essential
sparkwriters.org

Printed in Great Britain
by Amazon